Disney Princess

Cinderella

Disney
HACHETTE

Once upon a time in a faraway land there lived a beautiful girl called Cinderella. Her dearest friends were two little mice, called Jaq and Gus, and the songbirds who woke her up every morning with their dawn chorus.

Published by Hachette Partworks Ltd
ISBN: 978-1-906965-08-2
Date of Printing: December 2008
Printed in Singapore by Tien Wah Press

Cinderella's mother had died when she was young. Her father found a new wife, but he died too, so now Cinderella lived with her wicked stepmother and two stepsisters, Anastasia and Drizella, who treated her like a servant. The poor girl spent all day cooking, sewing, cleaning and dusting. The two lazy stepsisters never lifted a finger to help with the housework.

One day a royal messenger came to the house with a letter from the King. The Stepmother read it out: “There will be a ball in honour of His Royal Highness the Prince. By royal command, every eligible maiden is to attend.”

“That means I can go too!” exclaimed Cinderella. Anastasia and Drizella burst out laughing.

"Oh! Can't you just picture her, dancing with the Prince?" said Anastasia spitefully. She mocked Cinderella with glee. "Would your Highness be so good as to hold my broom?"

"But it says here that every girl in the kingdom must go," replied Cinderella.

"Well, there's no reason why you shouldn't go too," said the Stepmother slyly, "*if* you finish all your chores first and *if* you can find a suitable outfit to wear."

"Oh, thank you!" cried Cinderella, rushing to her bedroom.

Cinderella rummaged through an old trunk and pulled out a ballgown that had belonged to her mother. "It's a bit old-fashioned, but I'll soon fix that," she said. The little mice had never seen their dear friend look so happy.

Jaq and Gus were sure that Cinderella would be the belle of the ball!

Cinderella got out her sewing box. “I’ll need some ribbon and lace,” she said.

But just then, the Stepmother yelled: "Cinderella!"

The girl hurried downstairs.

"Cinderella, scrub the floor," the old lady barked.

"But I did that yesterday," protested Cinderella.

"Well, do it again," the cruel Stepmother insisted. "And then you can wash the curtains, clean the windows and finish cooking."

The little mice felt so sorry for their overworked friend.

"They've given her so many chores to do that she'll never find time to sew her dress," said Jaq.

"Poor Cinderelly," agreed Gus, shaking his head.

Then the mice had a brilliant idea – why didn't they finish Cinderella's dress for her?

So the mice and the birds got together and decided that they would all help their friend.

Gus and Jaq sneaked up to the stepsisters' bedroom as they were getting ready for the ball.

"This sash is so old," moaned Anastasia.

"And this necklace is hideous," shouted Drizella, as the two of them flung all their things on the floor.

Gus and Jaq saw their chance to sneak away with the necklace and the sash.

"Hurray!" cried Gus. "Shh!" hissed Jaq.

The two mice had to watch out for Lucifer the cat. Luckily they made it back to the attic safely.

Swiftly and skilfully, many nimble beaks and tiny paws went to work on Cinderella's gown. The animals set about measuring up, cutting and sewing, and while they were working...

... Cinderella was helping her two stepsisters to get ready for the ball.

Soon it was time to set off for the Palace.

"Cinderella! Why aren't you ready yet?" asked the Stepmother, pretending to be surprised. "You're far too late! We can't wait for you."

Cinderella climbed the stairs to her room sadly. Her gown wasn't ready and she couldn't go to the ball.

"Oh well," she said to herself, "what's all the fuss about a royal ball anyway? After all, it's bound to be very noisy, frightfully dull and terribly... wonderful."

Then Cinderella opened the bedroom door and...

"Surprise!" the birds and mice shouted together.

“I’ve never seen such a beautiful gown!” gasped Cinderella. “Thank you, thank you so much, all of you!”

In an instant Cinderella was ready and she raced downstairs to her stepsisters.

"Wait! Please! Wait for me!" she called.

"Mother, you can't allow this!" the stepsisters screamed.

“”Well girls, I suppose a promise is a promise,” said the Stepmother grudgingly.

But then Anastasia and Drizella recognised the old sash and necklace that the mice had taken from their room. They snatched them off Cinderella, tearing her gown into rags.

The poor girl ran crying into the garden. She was sure that her dreams would never come true now.

Her little friends had never seen Cinderella look so sad.

“I’ll never believe in dreams again,” Cinderella sobbed.

She was so busy crying that she didn’t notice a bright light shining around her. Jaq and Gus couldn’t believe their eyes as Cinderella’s Fairy Godmother appeared out of the light!

The Fairy Godmother stroked Cinderella's cheek: "Never again? You don't mean that," she said kindly.

"Dry those tears," she told Cinderella. "We must hurry, because even magic takes a little time!"

Everything the Fairy Godmother needed to help Cinderella was already in the garden.

"Bibbidi-bobbidi-boo!" commanded the Fairy Godmother, and in an instant the four mice were transformed into handsome white horses...

... the pumpkin turned into a beautiful coach, the horse became a smart coachman and Toby the dog was a footman!

Now it was Cinderella's turn.

"You can't go to the ball looking like that," said the Fairy Godmother, and with a wave of her magic wand, she changed Cinderella's rags into a beautiful ballgown. Cinderella loved her dress. "And look – glass slippers. Why, it's like a beautiful dream come true."

Then the Fairy Godmother warned the girl, "Don't forget that on the stroke of midnight the spell will be broken and everything will change back!"

Cinderella promised to return home before midnight and rushed off to the ball.

The ball had begun but the King was feeling sad.

He had planned the grand ball to find a bride for his son. But the Prince didn't seem to be interested in any of the girls there.

Suddenly Cinderella walked in and the instant he saw her, the Prince was in love. She was the girl of his dreams! He asked the mysterious girl to dance with him.

Cinderella accepted the Prince's offer and the couple danced gracefully around the ballroom to the tune of a beautiful waltz.

Everyone watched Cinderella in amazement.
"Do we know her?" asked Drizella.
"It looks as though the Prince might!" replied Anastasia.
"She does look rather familiar," said the Stepmother.

Once the dancing was over, the couple went for a walk in the garden.

Suddenly Cinderella heard the watchtower clock strike twelve.

"Oh no, it's midnight. I must go home!" she exclaimed.
"Wait!" the Prince called after her. But Cinderella kept running and as she ran, she lost one of her glass slippers.

The Prince showed the glass slipper to the Grand Duke.

"Find the girl who wore this slipper. She's the girl I want to marry!" he ordered.

Meanwhile, Cinderella's gown had changed back into rags. The coach was once again a pumpkin, the horses were mice, and the coachman and the footman weren't people any more. But Cinderella still held one of the glass slippers in her hand.

The Grand Duke searched the kingdom for the girl whose foot fit the slipper. Everyone knew that the Prince wanted to marry her.

Hearing the news, Cinderella gasped with joy and the Stepmother guessed the truth. She didn't want Cinderella to marry the Prince!

The Stepmother locked Cinderella in her bedroom, hiding the key in her pocket.

"We must rescue Cinderelly!" cried Gus and Jaq.

Using all their cunning, they managed to sneak the key from the Stepmother's pocket.

Then, after a hard struggle, they finally got the key to Cinderella.

They had to hurry. The Grand Duke was on his way to the house!

First, Anastasia tried in vain to cram her foot into the slipper.

Then it was Drizella's turn, but like her sister, her foot was too big.

The Grand Duke asked, "Are you the only maidens in this household?"

"There's no one else," replied the Stepmother. But just as the Grand Duke was turning to leave...

... Cinderella appeared, followed by Jaq and Gus.

"Wait, can I try it on too?" she asked. At that moment the wicked Stepmother tripped up the footman and the slipper fell to the floor and smashed!

But luckily Cinderella still had the other slipper, which fitted her perfectly.

So Cinderella and her handsome Prince were married, and everyone in the whole kingdom celebrated their wedding, especially Gus and Jaq.

At last, Cinderella's dreams had come true!